River Royals™

MASTER THE
MISSISSIPPI

Katie Clark & Sarah Wynne
Illustrated by Penny Weber

b bright sky press
HOUSTON, TEXAS

When I grow up, I'm going to be special.

Elizabeth Jane Bookman, the famous
macaroni, cheese and ketchup chef.
Dr. Bookman, putting Band-Aids® on everyone.
Or I could be a professional snorkeler.

Right now, I'm just Eliza Jane.

What I really want is to shine at school.

Miss Fletcher always asks Sally to answer questions in front of the class. Why doesn't she ask me? Maybe it's because Sally turns in her homework. I tried to finish mine in the bathtub, but a whale ate it.

Miss Fletcher thinks Sally is the Queen of Everything.

If I had a crown, I'd shine like Sally. I can hear Miss Fletcher now: "Eliza Jane, come in front of the class and tell us the answer."

Just imagine me, Eliza Jane, Queen of the Classroom.

"Today, we learn about the Mississippi River. It is the largest river in the United States," says Miss Fletcher.

I slide down in my chair and draw mermaids.

"The Mississippi River played an important role in American history. Civil War soldiers, European explorers and Native Americans lived along its banks," she says.

I count hairpins in her bun.

"The river flows through ten states before reaching the Port of New Orleans and the Gulf of Mexico," says Miss Fletcher. "New Orleans is famous for many things, such as the pirate Jean Lafitte, Creole cooking and a Mardi Gras celebration where they toss beads and crowns."

Crowns? If I go to New Orleans, I could get my crown and shine like Sally! Miss Fletcher will have to ask me to answer questions in front of the class.

"The source of the Mississippi River is the ankle-deep water of Minnesota's Lake Itasca," I hear Miss Fletcher say. "A raindrop falling in Lake Itasca would arrive at the Gulf of Mexico in ninety days."

Ninety days! Second grade will be over. I'll never get a chance to shine. How can I reach New Orleans faster than a raindrop?

My mom says my imagination
can take me anywhere.

What if I tubed the Mississippi?

I start daydreaming and begin to feel the
current. As my mind drifts, I grab a map and
my little brother Henry.

Lake Itasca, here we come!

WELCOME TO
Lake Itasca
MINNESOTA

Lake Itasca is bigger than my bathtub.

Where it changes from a lake into the
Mississippi River, we see wood frogs, river otters
and blue-spotted salamanders, but no mermaids.

Maybe it gets more interesting down the river.

Henry looks at the map.

"There's a roller coaster in a giant mall
to the south," he says. "Let's roll!"

I stop thinking about Lake Itasca when I hear Miss Fletcher say, "The Mississippi River flows through the Twin Cities of Minneapolis and St. Paul."

How are cities twins? Do they look alike? I wonder.

"They are called the Twin Cities because they are the two largest cities in Minnesota and sit on either side of the river," she says.

In the distance I spy a roller coaster bursting out of the Mall of America. The Mississippi River gets more exciting with each twist and turn.

I tell Henry, "This land was definitely made for you and me!"

"Say cheese," says Henry.
I smile for a picture.

"No, Eliza Jane, we're entering Wisconsin, the Land of Cheese," he says.

Back in the classroom, Miss Fletcher says, "Wisconsin is the dairy capital of the United States. More than one-and-a-half million cows make fifteen percent of our country's milk."

I want to thank those cows! Macaroni is all about Wisconsin cheese.

WELCOME TO
East Moline
ILLINOIS

Henry hears a train whistle. "The Rock
Island Line is up ahead. All aboard!" he says.

WELCOME TO
Rock Island
ILLINOIS

Rock Island Line

He's ready to ride, but I'm listening to
Miss Fletcher talk about the Quad Cities
on the Iowa-Illinois state line.

welcome to
BETTENDO
IOWA

"Iowa, the Hawkeye State, is part of our
'American Heartland,'" Miss Fletcher
says. "Iowa grows more corn than most
countries." She explains that irrigation
from the Mississippi River provides
water for all that corn.

WELCOME TO
DAVENPORT
IOWA

I see green tractors ahead on the map.
Henry loves tractors!

"Let's take a field trip to the
John Deere Headquarters in
Moline, Illinois," I say.

I am line leader. I don't make us walk
quietly or wear nametags. We learn
all about tractors, combines and
other farm machines from Mr. Deere.

Henry decides to stay and become
a farmer. I decide I'll put him in
time-out if he doesn't get off the
tractor. We decide to float south
to St. Louis, Missouri.

John Deere

Miss Fletcher says the
Gateway Arch in St. Louis is
America's tallest monument.

We sing, "Glory! Glory! Hallelujah!
Our tubes are floating on,"
as we drift under the giant arch.

"Eliza Jane," says Miss Fletcher, "Please stop singing."

Miss Fletcher teaches the class about the St. Louis
Cardinals. They are baseball players, not birds.
Henry wants to stay for a game, but he notices
there are racehorses in the next state on the map.

Sure enough, we see a horse on the riverbank in Columbus, Kentucky. Her name is Royal Duchess. She hopes to run in the three most important races in America to win the Triple Crown.

"Poor pony. I know where to get you a crown, maybe even three. Come with us to New Orleans for the Mardi Gras parade," I say.

She whinnies and gallops into the river.

"Eliza Jane, are you listening?" I hear Miss Fletcher say. "You seem miles away."

"The Mississippi River is also used for transportation," she says. "Boats and barges move cargo to the Gulf of Mexico, where it is shipped all over the world."

While Miss Fletcher talks about cargo, the waves from a barge push us into the riverbank. A man in a sequined eagle jumpsuit says "Welcome to Memphis, Tennessee. You kids look all shook up!"

"Are you the King of Rock and Roll?" Henry asks.

"No, I'm just Melvis. I need a crown to be the king."

"We need crowns, too! Come with us to New Orleans," I tell him. "A crown will make you shine like the real king."

He tightens his blue suede shoes and shimmies into the river.

"It's now or never," he sings.

We rock all the way to Helena, Arkansas. Miss Fletcher says Arkansas is the only state that mines diamonds.

"Diamonds would make our crowns—and my jumpsuit—shine even brighter!" says Melvis. He gets so excited he starts to sing.

"Shh," I tell him. "We need to listen to Miss Fletcher. She's talking about Mark Twain. He was a writer with a big imagination and a sense of humor." I think I would like Mr. Mark Twain.

"Did you write about queens?" I ask him as we float by.

"No, child," he says, "but I've written stories about this mighty river. Her waters gleam like Tom Sawyer's freshly white-washed fence. In this country you don't need crowns to shine. The strength of America lies in the hearts and dreams of her people."

"Thank you, Mr. Twain," we say, minding our manners.

"See you in the library," I call back to him.

"I wish I was in the land of cotton,"
Melvis serenades us.

Henry studies the map and says, "Wait! We *are* in King Cotton,
the great State of Mississippi."

Miss Fletcher's voice brings me back
to the classroom.

"Cotton is used in products we use everyday,
including clothing, plastics, fertilizer, fuel
and paper," she says.

Then I hear another voice.

"I do declare," says a real Southern belle. "Welcome to Natchez, Mississippi. I'm Savannah Grace."

"Thank you, Miss Savannah," I say. "Are you the Mississippi Queen?"

"No, my dear. I entered the Miss Delta Queen pageant, but someone else won the crown," she says.

"Bless your heart," I say. "I know where to get you a crown, without a swimsuit competition."

Savannah Grace giggles and says, "Oh, fiddle-de-dee, for tomorrow's another day!" She curtsies and sashays into the river.

Henry rolls his eyes. "Girls!"

Then he perks up. "I see a football stadium ahead on the map. Float on to Baton Rouge, Louisiana!"

Drifting by the stadium, we hear the
roar of the crowd. It sounds like wild
animals at the zoo.

"That's no hound dog, that's a tiger! Let's shake, rattle and
roll out of here!" sings Melvis.

There's so much to do along the Mississippi, but we still need our
crowns. Will we ever get there? We must be getting closer, because
I hear Miss Fletcher talking about New Orleans.

"The Mississippi River connects major cities, including Minneapolis,
St. Louis, Memphis, Baton Rouge and New Orleans," she says.

She just said New Orleans! We're here!

"I feel my temperature rising!" sings Melvis.

Brown pelicans, barges and large ships pass us as we head into port. Jazz music and the yummy smell of beignets fill the air.

We jump on Royal Duchess. She gallops down Royal Street past colorful costumes, flying beads, floats, musicians and cheering crowds.

Our royal moment has arrived!

The parade's Grand Marshall says, "Come on up to the front."
He crowns us the Kings and Queens of Mardi Gras.

"Time to celebrate with King's Cake!"
Henry shouts. I wonder if it tastes
good with ketchup.

I do my queenie wave: elbow, elbow, wrist, wrist. Royal Duchess races through the streets. Savannah Grace and Henry toss beads. Melvis rocks the crowd.

We feel as important as Sally, as fast as a Triple Crown winner, as famous as a rock star and as pretty as a beauty queen!

But not for long...

The Grand Marshall tosses crowns to everyone in the crowd. No one is more important than anyone else.

I look at Henry and my new friends. We don't shine any brighter with crowns.

I remember what Mr. Twain said. In our country, we don't need crowns. What makes us special lies in our hearts and dreams. *We the People* make America shine.

I can't wait to share everything I've learned with my class, even Sally.

A familiar voice interrupts my daydream.

"Eliza Jane. Eliza Jane! Have you heard a word I said? Can you tell me the path of the Mississippi River?" asks Miss Fletcher.

"Yes!" I answer. "I've mastered the Mississippi! The river is really exciting, even without mermaids. Let me tell you about my trip."

"Your trip?" asks Miss Fletcher. She smiles, shakes her head and invites me to the front of the class.

I tell my friends about the amazing people who live and work along the Mississippi. Quaint little towns and big cities all work together to make America shine.

"United we stand," I say. Then I burst into song, "And crown thy good with brotherhood, from Lake Itasca to shining sea!"

I'm not a queen of anything, but I love America!

MISS FLETCHER'S MAP

I think I'm ready for another river adventure.

MISSISSIPPI
River Facts

Continent: North America

Path: The Mississippi River flows through ten states in the United States: Minnesota, Wisconsin, Iowa, Illinois, Missouri, Kentucky, Tennessee, Arkansas, Mississippi and Louisiana.

Length: The Mississippi River runs approximately 2,530 miles (4,071 km). It's the largest river in the United States and fifth largest river in the world by volume.

Width: At its widest point, the Mississippi River stretches more than seven miles (11 km) in width.

Source: The river starts as ankle-deep water in Lake Itasca, Minnesota.

Mouth: The river ends in the Gulf of Mexico after flowing through New Orleans, Louisiana.

Habitats: Many different kinds of wildlife make their homes in or near the river, including 241 species of fish, 37 species of mussels, 45 amphibians, 50 mammals and 40 percent of the United States' migratory birds.

History: The river has historical significance to Native Americans, European explorers and American Civil War soldiers.

Literature: The river is the subject of Mark Twain's classic novel, *Huckleberry Finn*.

Fun Record: In 2002, Martin Strel, a Slovenian swimmer, swam the entire length of the river in 68 days.

Fun Fact: A raindrop falling in Lake Itasca would arrive at the Gulf of Mexico in 90 days!